THE SMALL WAR OF SERGEANT DONKEY

Also by Maureen Daly

Seventeenth Summer
Sixteen and Other Stories
The Ginger Horse

The Small War of Sergeant Donkey

By
Maureen Daly

Illustrated by
Wesley Dennis

BETHLEHEM BOOKS • IGNATIUS PRESS
BATHGATE, N.D.   SAN FRANCISCO

Cover art © 2000 by Lydia Halverson
Cover design by Davin Carlson

Interior artwork by Wesley Dennis

First Bethlehem Books edition, September 2000

ISBN 1–883937–47–7
Library of Congress Control Number: 00–101260

Bethlehem Books • Ignatius Press
10194 Garfield Street South
Bathgate, ND 58216
www.bethlehembooks.com

Printed in the United States on acid free paper

For my good friend, Major John Burkholder,
formerly of the U.S. Army Remount Division in Italy,
with thanks for his enthusiasm, patience—and memories

CHICO FILIPPO lay flat on the dusty grass, resting his chin on his folded arms. It was late afternoon, and from the village of San Palio, a half mile away, he heard the distant sound of church bells ringing out the Angelus.

Since a German mortar shell had knocked off the top of the church belfry, five months ago, the old bells had a new sound, a thin, clanging peal, almost as if they were frightened. They toned out now over the flat farm lands and echoed in the wooded mountains that were set in a half-ring around the valley. Chico counted out the chimes as they rang . . . four, five, six. Six o'clock. Time for the evening prayer. Before her death, some years before, his mother had taught young Chico how to pray. Dutifully he made the sign of the cross on his forehead, murmured a few words of the Angelus prayer, and then rolled over on his back to stare at the blue Italian sky,

1

turning a gray-pink at the horizon with the first touches of a November dusk.

Above him, the broad, green leaves of a gnarled old fig tree were patterned against the light, moving gently in the wind that swept down from the mountains. Chico sighed. It was hard to be happy in wartime, even though the sky was still clear and the earth still warm and comforting against his thin young shoulders.

Chico knew that next month the winter rains would begin; hard, slanting rains that runneled down the cobblestone streets of the village, beat against the stone walls of the houses, and turned their marble floors into chill dampness. In the evening, his nineteen-year-old sister, Annalisa, would cook the supper over a tiny, flickering fire of charcoal or a handful of the pine cones he had gathered on the mountainsides all summer and stored in the root cellar under the house. In his mind, Chico could almost smell the thin odor of a vegetable stew or a half-warmed soup, floating with bits of dried mushroom and shreds of cabbage, a few drops of rich olive oil glistening on top. A cupful of soup each for himself, Annalisa, and his little brother and sister. With every winter, there was less to simmer on the little iron stove.

It was 1944, the fifth November of World War II in Italy, a long, long time in Chico's memory, almost one-third of his twelve years of life. Sometimes it seemed to him that his country had always been at

war. He remembered all too clearly the day most of the young and stronger men of the village of San Palio, his father among them, had marched off to join the Italian army. Then, months later, the Germans had taken command, with thousands of well-equipped, uniformed troops sweeping down from the north of Italy to occupy all the major towns and seaports, set up gun positions in the mountains, and turn his country into a German-controlled garrison, even down to his own little village.

And then, last year, the tide of the war had begun to change. The sky, the earth—all of Chico's world—had been filled with the fierce air and land fighting, as American and British troops battled their way up from the south of Italy, pushing back the Germans town by town, valley by valley, mountain by mountain.

Most of the heavy fighting was over now in Chico's part of southern Italy, but sometimes, late in the night, as he lay in his narrow bed, the boy thought he still heard distant artillery fire echoing far off in the mountains. Half asleep, he never felt sure whether it was real gunfire or just frightened memories come to shake terror into his dreams.

Lying now in the grass, his fingers touched an overripe fig, soft but leathery, one of the last to fall from the tree. Raising himself on his elbow, Chico picked up the fruit and blew off a small striped wasp feasting on the oozing juice. Carefully, he bit into the fruit, chewing slowly to enjoy the sweet softness of the pink flesh with its tiny brown seeds, savoring even the wrinkled skin that was black and tough as licorice.

Chico was hungry, really hungry, and it was a long walk back to his house, just on the outskirts of the old village.

Every day for more than a month he had come in the late afternoon to lie in the grass outside the new American barracks. His curiosity grew stronger each time he came. It began in early October, just after the last German machine-gun nest around the ancient abbey at the top of the mountains had been wiped out. A company of American soldiers had arrived by truck and jeep and set up camp on the old animal market grounds outside San Palio.

Before the war, and even far back before Chico was born, farmers from the whole valley and from the villages beyond the mountains had gathered twice a year, driving their farm animals before them, to buy and sell stock at the San Palio animal market.

Since their arrival one bright fall morning, the American troops had made many changes in the market grounds. The rough old pens for the goats and sheep still stood; the paddocks, fenced with split pine from the mountains, that had herded in the donkeys and mules, were still in use, but the soldiers had fenced in several dozen more acres with pine posts and barbed wire. On the far side of the grounds, the sagging, weather-worn stock sheds had been patched up and re-roofed and the Americans had added a number of low, rambling buildings, painted white and facing the cobblestone courtyard with its old stone well and pump. The new buildings were administration offices, barracks for sleeping, a cookhouse, mess hall, blacksmith shop, and a hospital building with a staff of veterinarians and special stalls and paddocks for sick animals.

The front gate of the market grounds was guarded now at all times by two armed soldiers and from dawn to dusk an American flag fluttered over the new encampment. Posted over the main gate was a freshly painted sign: U. S. ARMY REMOUNT DEPOT.

Chico knew many words of English, some from hearing soldiers talk in the village, and others from school classes before the war, but the sign meant nothing to him. All he knew about the project was what he saw with his own eyes: in just a few weeks, the Americans had hammered, sawed, painted, sunk fence posts, and strung wire to make a big, efficient camp for themselves—and for hundreds of assorted donkeys and mules.

The first loads of mules had come in by open army truck. The animals, almost as big as full-grown horses, stood upright in the back of the trucks, legs braced wide, long, sensitive ears raised. As truck after truck bounced over the rough-stoned streets, the quiet of the village was shattered by their harsh braying.

Later, the donkeys began to arrive in droves and were driven into the valley by soldiers on horseback, like herds of cattle, their sharp little hoofs kicking up a thick dust as they trotted over the dry fields toward the new paddocks.

At the end of ten days, the corrals were crowded with dusty, shuffling, milling, braying mules and donkeys. The mules, larger and longer legged, were mostly a flat brownish-gray in color, while the donkeys ranged in coat from a dark brown, through dark gray and light silver, to those with a silken-stubble hide that was almost white. Chico quickly lost count of the number of animals in the pens but he guessed that altogether there must be at least a thousand. And each day, new animals arrived.

And each afternoon, Chico came to lie in the grass and observe the sturdy, four-legged creatures, well watered and well fed, milling about in the enclosures. He watched the animals with almost breathless fascination. There was a strength in their muscled movements and a familiar animal warmth and smell that attracted and comforted the boy.

Before the war, Chico's father had been a farmer, living in the village and farming a half-dozen fields just outside town. He had owned two strong little donkeys with broad backs and stout legs to plow the fields, help harvest the crops, and carry fresh produce into the village square on market day. Each day the donkeys worked; each night they were stabled in a small, snug shed just behind the house. These burros seemed as much a part of the Filippo family as Chico's grandfather or the newest baby.

But the donkeys, along with all the other work beasts of the village, had been confiscated by the German army nearly three years ago. Ever since, the shed had stood bare and empty and farm fields had lain idle and unplowed, except for a small plot that Chico himself dug up with a spade. For three years there had been no vegetables to sell in the village market.

After the two donkeys, the family's flock of sheep had disappeared, animal by animal. For years, as regular as the rooster's crow, Chico's grandfather had started at daybreak to guide the sheep up into the mountains to pasture. Just before sunset, he would begin the trek down again, the big tin bells on the lead rams echoing out like tinkling music over the valley. In the summertime, ever since he was a small boy, Chico had helped his grandfather to tend the sheep, wandering over narrow paths from one grassy plateau to another until he knew the mountain trails as well as he knew the crooked little streets of his own village.

But the Germans had wanted those sheep. When they first arrived in San Palio, the tender young lambs were slaughtered as food for the troops. Later, most of the older sheep were also confiscated. Then two summers ago, when the mountains above the village were bristling with German gun positions and pitted with land mines, all villagers were ordered to stay out of the upper pasture lands. The few sheep still left foraged for food on the dry plains or nibbled at the scraggly bushes just outside the village.

As the war grew longer and food supplies grew shorter, the last skinny, dusty sheep was used for food. The spirits of Chico's grandfather seemed to weaken and wane with the flock. Last winter, the old man became ill and lingered silently under worn blankets in a back bedroom until one morning—just at sun-up—he died. He seemed to have become too saddened by the changes of war to stay alive any longer.

Lying now in the grass, Chico's thoughts yearned toward the healthy, milling animals inside the paddocks. He listened to their movements, sniffed at the exciting animal-scented air. For a moment, he felt as safe, as peaceful, almost as well fed as he had before the war.

The boy closed his eyes, pretending that the clip-clop of hoofs was sounding in his own stable yard behind the house. His daydream seemed suddenly to come alive, shot through with a dozen prewar memories of times when life was good: the garlands of hot peppers his mother and Annalisa used to string up each fall to dry in the sun near the front door; his father's wet boots drying under the iron stove in winter, broad leather toes curling with the heat; his grandfather whittling a whistle of aspen wood up on the mountainside; the two family donkeys, washed and curried, harnesses braided and bowed with ribbons, drawing a cart holding the flower-crowned Statue of the Virgin through the village on holy feast days. . . . Without war, there was so much good to remember.

* * *

"Now I lay me down to sleep, I pray the Lord my soul to keep. . . ."

Chico opened his eyes and sat up with a start, feeling at once an evening chill in the air. He realized he had fallen asleep. Now, staring down at him from the other side of the barbed wire, was an American soldier, a tall, brawny young man with hair the color of ripe wheat and skin as sunburned and weathered as a gypsy's. His big hands, resting on the top wire strand, were ridged with muscles and tanned the same leather-brown as his face.

"I do nothing wrong," Chico said quickly.

"Course not," the young soldier assured him. "I just saw you snoozing off for the night and I was tucking you in with a prayer, like we do back home."

Chico brushed his hand over his eyes and smoothed back his black hair to show he was wide-awake. Then he got to his feet and shyly, carefully thinking out each word, said, "I just come to look at mules and donkeys. So *many.*"

The soldier turned to glance over the animals in the corral in which he stood and then let his eyes rove over the other crowded paddocks. "Dang right, there's a lot," he agreed thoughtfully, "and more coming in the day after tomorrow."

"More!" Chico echoed, his voice small with awe. "Even *more?*"

"Yes, we've got a good stock of those little fellows," the soldier told him, pointing out some of the stout brown donkeys in the paddock behind him. "But we're waiting for a shipload of the big boys to come in from Missouri."

"*Big boys?*" Chico asked, puzzled. He stared hard at the soldier, almost hoping to read the meaning of the words in his friendly, sun-tanned face. At that moment Chico desperately wished he knew more English. "*Big boys!*"

"Big mules, I mean," the soldier explained. "We've rounded up all the mules we can get our hands on here in southern Italy and we captured a good many from the Germans as they pulled out. Lots they just left running free. But we need more. Now we've

started shipping animals all the way over from the States. Big old Missouri mules."

The tall soldier looked thoughtful for a moment, his blue eyes with their sandy lashes almost closed. Then he said softly, "I'm from Missouri myself. Some of those mules might be coming right from my part of the country." He stood quiet for a moment, staring out over the dusty valley as if he were thinking of something far away. "Big old Missouri mules," he repeated softly.

Chico waited, feeling suddenly very shy and awkward in his tattered shorts and worn shirt, his bare feet scuffed and grubby with dirt. Even though his khaki shirt showed signs of the hard work he had been doing, the big soldier looked neat and trim, with his shirt sleeves folded back almost to his three sergeant's stripes, khaki trousers tucked into stout, heavy-soled boots laced up above the ankle. Chico put his hands self-consciously into his ragged pockets but they slipped right through the worn linings to touch his scrawny bare legs.

He paused for a moment, trying to keep the sound of shame out of his voice. It was hard to talk when one felt so shabby and so small, but the boy was torn with curiosity.

"Will you make big farms here, you American soldiers?" he asked. "With so many big animals for the plow, you will make big fields everywhere?"

The soldier looked at him for a moment and then laughed aloud. "No, sir," he answered firmly. "These animals aren't for farming. These mules and donkeys, why—they're serving right in the United States Army!"

"Soldier donkeys!" Chico exclaimed, unbelieving.

The sergeant nodded. "Soldier donkeys—and mules. Some of them have seen a lot of action already. Before we captured them, the Germans nearly worked the hide off half those jenny mules, hauling supply carts and munitions out of Austria and down into Italy.

"And a lot of the little fellows, those work donkeys, hauled everything from medicine to ammunition for our troops down in North Africa. Maybe those little African burros *look* small but they're strong as the devil and work like . . . well, like donkeys!"

"And never pull plows at all?" Chico asked.

"Not till this war is over," the sergeant answered. "The Apennine Mountains run right up and down the middle of this country like a big backbone. That means we've got to beat the Germans in mountain fighting here to win our war. A pack train of these little burros can carry food, medicine, or munitions on narrow back roads or up and down mountain trails where no horse or truck could go. Trucks and tanks can make it on the highways, but in the mountains and back country, these little donkeys are the heroes. A good work donkey is so sure-footed he walks as though he's got brains in his feet. . . ."

"But there is no more war *here*," said Chico, gesturing toward the mountains and the plains outside San Palio.

"That's right," agreed the sergeant. "But there's

still plenty of fighting up north. The Germans hold everything from a hundred miles south of Rome on up. We don't have them licked yet.

"We set up our depot at San Palio so we can get the animals sorted out and trained and sent up north fast. If they're sick, the vets here fix them up. We give them all a workout to see which ones are good in a pack train, who's stubborn, and who'll take orders. Before they get sent north, we have to know which animals will make good soldiers."

"Good soldiers?" Chico said, his voice still puzzled.

The sergeant nodded. "Every day we pick out enough mules or donkeys for a half dozen or more pack trains. We put them in full harness, load up the saddle sacks to see how much weight they're willing to carry, and then take them up in these mountains for a workout.

"It's training, or like a checkup. We find out who wants to follow the leader, who's balky, who's willing to haul a good load. And we find out who's got sure feet on those mountain trails and who knows how to keep his mouth shut. Nobody's got much use for a donkey that might start to heehaw and holler when there are Germans around. Some got the habit of singing out for no reason at all. We need animals that can do a *soldiering* job. Once we know what an animal's worth and what he can do, he's sent up north to get in the action."

The soldier reached down to pat the muzzle of a

big gray mule grazing beside him. "A lot of good soldiers wouldn't be alive today without the supplies these jenny mules pulled through. For speed and strength, give me a mule. But for a trip where there's trouble—like bad roads or the mountains after dark— I'll bet my money on a good little donkey."

At that moment a small donkey, so light in color it seemed to shine silver-white, hobbled over and nuzzled at the sergeant's hand. The young American laughed and rubbed the beast gently on the flat, broad space between its eyes. The silver-white eyelashes almost closed. The burro hobbled closer until its flank rubbed against the khaki trousers, the broad back of the animal barely reaching to the soldier's waistline.

"He is so *small*," said Chico softly. "Small like a baby."

"Small but no baby," the sergeant told him. "This little fellow is probably three or four years old and in his full growth. He's a North African donkey. Most of them are this light color, and small in size."

"Is he big enough to be a soldier donkey?" Chico asked.

"He's a real little soldier," the sergeant answered. "And a brave one. He trekked munitions all through the Lybian and Egyptians deserts, right up to El Alamein. Then he got sent up here. And see that broken leg?" He pointed to the right back leg.

Chico moved nearer to the fence and examined the little animal more closely. One back leg was braced with a steel splint, in front and behind, heavily taped and bandaged into place. The burro hobbled easily on three legs, favoring his injured limb.

"About three weeks ago, we were unloading a ship-load of these little African fellows over in Naples Harbor. There were only about eight of us doing the job because the United States Army doesn't have too many farm boys that are good mule handlers. We were working on the double, taking out the donkeys from the hold, three at a time instead of one," the sergeant explained.

"Regular as clockwork, a couple of German Luft-waffe planes would come in low and strafe the docks and everything in sight." He pointed to the burro. "This little fellow was just being unloaded with two other donkeys. They were hanging in mid-air half-way over the dock in a big cargo net, when the planes flew in. We all ducked for shelter, and this donkey just hung there for a good ten minutes or more, bullets flying around. But he never made a sound—not even when a bullet nicked him in the hock. The other two donkeys in the net were shot dead."

Chico felt a surge of sympathy. He remembered his own intense fear, hiding in the root cellar be-neath the house with Annalisa and his little brother and sister when the American Army first arrived and German mortars shelled the town for three straight days. And this little donkey hadn't even cried out.

"The major wanted to shoot him right there," said

the soldier. "To put him out of his misery. But I took a hankering to the little fellow and the major let me take him on as a kind of pet. I just figured if he survived the Luftwaffe, he was *meant* to stay alive.

"The vet set his leg and we believe in a week or so he'll be good as new. That burro's a tough one, all right."

The sun had sunk so low in the sky that the shadow of the old fig tree stretched long and cast leafy patterns right into the paddock. Chico remembered suddenly how hungry he was and the long walk back home, but he did not want to seem impolite by hurrying away. Instead, he gave a little bow from the waist and said formally to the soldier, "I *like* to speak with you. Thank you. My name is Chico, Chico Filippo."

The big soldier put out his hand and said, "Glad to meet you, Chico. I'm Sergeant Price. John Price. But most of the time I'm just called 'Missouri.' "

"Sergeant Missouri," Chico replied politely. Then, turning to the little white burro, he made a mock bow and said, "And Sergeant Donkey." The soft muzzle quivered and Chico put his hand through the barbed wire to rub the small donkey on its nose.

*   *   *

For the next three days, Chico had no time at all to go to the Remount Depot, and little time to think about the donkeys and mules. He himself felt like a work beast. On the first day, Annalisa had climbed with him to the roof of their house, pointing out just where the tiles were broken and where they could expect leaks in the winter rains. On the slanting roof over the kitchen, leafed over with a mass of blue-flowered morning glories, she pulled back vines and leaves to show him a hole as big as his hand.

Since there was no money for new tiles, Chico spent the morning carefully removing whole tiles from one side of the old stable. With no animals to house, it would matter little if half the stable leaked. The sun was just showing its last light in the crooked streets of the village when he clambered down wearily from the roof of the house, every hole and crack carefully re-covered.

On the next day, he left at sunrise with a spade in hand, burlap sack over his shoulder, and his six-year-old brother at his heels. They trudged out to the farm field where Chico had so carefully spaded up a garden in the spring. Most of the tomatoes, peppers, zucchini, and white squash had already been harvested and eaten during the summer months. Part of that crop had been used in trade with the village merchants for yeast, matches, olive oil, spools of thread—simple things that Annalisa needed to run the house.

Today, Chico dug out the carrots, parsnips, big onions, and the few potatoes that still remained in the ground. The double row of coarse, long-leafed cabbages could stand where they were during the cold and winter rains, ready to be cut when needed.

The older boy dug, while his brother collected the vegetables, shook off the mud, and stuffed them into the big sack. It took Chico six weary journeys, the heavy sack slung over his shoulder and banging against the back of his knees, to get the vegetables home and into the root cellar under the house. Here Annalisa carefully packed the produce in heaps of damp sand to keep them fresh and so insure the family of *some* food supply for the cold winter months.

As he climbed into bed that night, the palms of Chico's hands smarted with blisters from the spading and his legs ached right down to his ankles, but he fell asleep dreaming of butter and a fat slab of smoked bacon and plump chickens to simmer in a pot with potatoes and carrots.

On the third day, Chico rose early to get ready for his long hike up the mountains to the abbey. Every few weeks, Father Antonio—the local parish priest—asked him to carry up some scant supplies to the three old monks still living in the Abbey of San Isidro. Most of the time, Father Antonio, as poor as the other villagers, had nothing himself to send except a newspaper from Rome or a worn book off his own shelves. But before each trip, Chico made the rounds of the village shops, a knapsack strapped to his back, to beg for the Brothers.

Today, with much grumbling, the baker gave him two pounds of white flour. At the general store, the proprietor added three wax candles and a ball of twine. The pharmacy owner contributed a jar of spicy wintergreen ointment "guaranteed to cure anything," and the owner of one café added a bottle of red wine, just a little sour, and a tin of anchovies that had been bought in Naples even before the war. The butcher contributed two soup bones wrapped in newspaper and promised a couple of stewing rabbits the next time. Annalisa herself added a half dozen of the precious vegetables from the cellar and three pairs of socks which she had made by painstakingly unraveling Grandfather's old sweater and reknitting the gray wool.

Just before noon, Chico crossed the fields of the open valley and began his climb up the mountain. By habit, he now chose the winding, little-used trails—even though they made the journey longer. Ever since the Germans had first come to San Palio, he had kept away from main pathways and the trails worn through the woods by decades of flocks and shepherds. To Chico, light and agile as a deer, the mountains were as old friends.

The Abbey of San Isidro, situated as it was on a rocky peak, with miles of mountainsides and valley spread out before it, and with an almost unclimbable precipice dropping down hundreds of feet from its back wall, had made a near-perfect fortress for the Germans. Early in their occupation of Italy, the German command had sent all but five of the abbey's monks up to Rome. Troops had occupied the abbey and the centuries-old walls bristled with machine guns and mortars until San Isidro became an armed lookout point, commanding the whole valley.

When the American and British troops began to push north, the walled abbey seemed almost impregnable. It took weeks of aerial bombing and hard infantry fighting, as the Allied soldiers inched their way up the mountainsides under a nearly constant barrage of mortar fire. When the remnants of the German garrison finally surrendered, San Isidro was a near shambles of crumbled walls and shattered buildings.

Two of the monks had died in the bombardments but the last three had been saved, almost miraculously, even though they were kneeling in prayer in the chapel the night the north wall had been blasted in on them. They had continued to chant their prayers, even as the windows were shattered and shards of the colored stained glass covered the ancient altar like glistening flower petals.

After the last Germans had been taken prisoner, the American command allowed the three old monks to stay on at San Isidro, living as well as they could from the meager produce of the abbey garden or what they could salvage from the debris. Now, for Brother Gregorio, Brother Massimo, and Brother Honeycake, young Chico was the only contact with the outside world.

As he slipped softly through the cool shadows of the mountain forests, with the knapsack secure on his back, Chico found himself smiling at his own thoughts. In the old days—the bright, sunny days before the war—the abbey had been an important part of San Palio village life. Its great stone cross, now crumbled under mortar fire, had been built of a shiny quartz stone that caught and sent back the sunlight like chunks of sparkling diamonds. The cross of San Isidro, higher than the mountain peak itself, had seemed like a beacon light, a symbol of protection for all the valley.

And year after year, on the first Sunday in May, whole families of villagers made the long trek up to San Isidro, dressed in their Sunday best and laden with picnic baskets and carafes of wine. After hearing Mass sung in honor of the Holy Virgin, they spread their lunches out on the grass inside the abbey walls and the feasting and laughing lasted almost until sundown.

It was then that Brother Honeycake passed out to every child on the pilgrimage his famous heart-shaped cookies, crisp little cakes he made himself and flavored sweetly with wild honey. At the far end of the abbey garden, Brother Honeycake kept a score of beehives and the honey, gathered from mountain flowers, had a special sweet and scented flavor. His religious name was Brother Anselmo, but to Chico, and to every child raised in the village of San Palio for nearly the last half century, this old monk—the keeper of the bees—was known as Brother Honeycake.

The sun was nearly at the high point of noon when Chico reached the entrance to the abbey, with its great carved doors hanging open on rusted iron hinges. Giving a shrill whistle between his teeth, the same sharp whistle with which shepherds call to their goats and sheep, Chico went inside. Brothers Gregorio and Massimo were just about to be seated for their noonday meal at an old table set up in the kitchen. Brother Honeycake came in from the gardens, his worn breviary clasped in his hand.

Chico, hungry after his long trek, gratefully accepted the Brothers' invitation to join them and stood with head bowed while Brother Gregorio intoned a long prayer of thanksgiving and Brother Honeycake went to fetch another bowl and spoon. However, as he drank his soup, Chico felt there was very little to be thankful for. Thick and dark orange in color, he realized, to his intense distaste, that the Brothers were eating a soup made of boiled, mashed pumpkin.

"Perhaps next time you might manage to bring some salt," Brother Massimo said apologetically. "I am a teacher of Latin classics, really—not a cook. But I know that soup should have salt."

The others nodded and drank on in silence.

*　　*　　*

After a final prayer of thanksgiving, Chico opened his knapsack and laid out the meager gifts of the village. The Brothers were warm in their thanks, and then Brother Honeycake announced, proudly, that he had a gift to send back to the town. On each visit, this routine was exactly the same. Carrying his knapsack Chico followed Brother Honeycake out to the beehives. The old monk carefully lined the knapsack with fresh green leaves, then took six combs of sweet honey from the hives and packed them in the canvas bag. As always, Chico voiced his thanks for Brother Honeycake's generosity and promised to deliver the gift to Father Antonio at the village church that very evening. With sugar, candy, chocolate, or any sweet whatever almost completely unavailable for months and months, Father Antonio was in charge of distributing the honey to those who needed it most—to the very old or the sick, and sometimes to little children especially peaked and pinched from chronic undernourishment. Chico strapped on the knapsack carefully, knowing he carried a small treasure on his back.

Brother Honeycake walked with him across the vast, rubble-strewn courtyard as far as the old front gate. There the beloved monk stood to wave as the boy began the steep climb back down the trail. Chico remembered how it had been in the old days when he and his grandfather had visited the abbey. Often they came up to trade goat's-milk cheeses for honey and stayed on to lunch with the monks at a long table in the ancient refectory hall, now a crumble of ruins. Chico remembered a table spread with good food and plates piled high with crisp bread, still warm from the oven. Then, too, Brother Honeycake had liked to walk with them to the front gate and he always stood for a moment to puff a few times on Grandfather's twisted black cigar.

"I promised to obey God in vows of poverty, obedience, and no women," Brother Honeycake would say, "but He forgot to make a rule about smoking." The old shepherd would laugh and slap his brawny thigh at the comic sight of the squat little monk, solemn in brown robes and cowl, blowing cigar smoke out of his nostrils.

After his grandfather's death, Chico had made the sad climb to tell the Brothers the news and to ask for prayers for the old man's soul. Before leaving the village, he had traded a big head of cabbage at the tobacco shop for two of his grandfather's favorite cigars. On that trip, at the front-gate farewell, he had offered the cigars to Brother Honeycake, who shook his head and said, "No, no, Chicito. Not for me. Never again. I only smoked to hear my old friend laugh."

Absorbed in his own thoughts, Chico moved swiftly down the rocky, wooded trails, hardly needing to watch where he was going, enjoying the clear air and the sharp smell of pine when his sandals slipped and crushed the needles that bedded over the paths. About halfway down, he stopped to rest, choosing a flat plateau, a treeless stretch of soft, lush grass, open to the sunlight. He and his grandfather had often spent whole days at this spot, letting the sheep graze and feed as they pleased. Backed by woods, one side of the plateau was open to a sharp, rocky drop. Beyond was a stretch of rough mountain land, with stony trails and a dry stream bed winding through sparse trees and ending at a deep chasm about twelve feet across.

Chico lay down now on the soft grass, settling carefully on his stomach, so as not to crush the knapsack of honey on his back. The usual hunger gnawing at him had been silenced by the pumpkin soup and the afternoon had a sun-warmed, drowsy quality. "I must be careful not to drop off to sleep," he thought.

Then, suddenly, his whole body and senses became alerted by one of the strangest sights he had ever seen. Surprise, sheer shock, kept him silent as he stared. Far below, but coming toward him on a narrow, rocky path, was a line of brown donkeys, each saddled with double panniers, or baskets, of sturdily woven straw, loaded with heavy stones. Every donkey wore flat, brown blinders fastened to the bridle at the side of his eyes. The hoofs of all the beasts were bound and padded with rolls of cloth. There were eight donkeys in all and Chico saw that two of them had their muzzles bound firmly shut with a band of cloth between the eyes and nostrils.

At the head of the donkey train walked a soldier. A second soldier followed in the rear. Each man was helmeted and uniformed in the smudged and dappled green-and-brown coloring of camouflage cloth. Except for the automatic rifles slung across their backs, Chico wondered if he would have seen the men at all, so effectively did they merge with sun and shadow.

The strangeness of the sight was made more eerie by its silence. The donkeys seemed to be walking on velvet feet. The first soldier directed the lead donkey without a spoken word, commanding him to stop by touching him lightly on the nose with a short stick, then ordering him to proceed ahead with a sharp poke at his haunch. And the other seven donkeys, eyes straight ahead, stopped and started in docile obedience. Closer and closer, up the steep path, the strange company climbed. Once they halted for a full five minutes, neither men nor donkeys making a movement or sound. It seemed as if even breathing stopped. The concentration and intensity of both men and beasts held Chico spellbound. At one point, the strange procession passed almost beneath him. He could stare down from his grassy plateau and see the loaded donkeys parade under his eyes.

With the same noiseless precision, the caravan reached the edge of the chasm and the lead donkey was halted by the signal to his nose. The seven other well-trained beasts came to a standstill behind him. Without a word, the first soldier began to unpack gear from the panniers on the lead donkey. He tied one end of a stout rope around a pine tree and then, with the skill of a practiced cowhand, he whirled a loop of rope over the chasm, lassoing it firmly onto a jutting rock on the other side. Then carefully, hand over hand, he inched his way over the open gorge, to clamber safely up on the other side.

Now the second soldier untied the rope from the

pine tree and attached it to a strange bundle that had been unloaded from a pannier. The first soldier began pulling on his end of the rope, slowly and carefully, to unroll and pull over the chasm a five-foot-wide roll of metal slats, flexible but strong and bound together at the sides with heavy chains. After ten minutes of intense labor, still without a word spoken, Chico realized that the two men had erected a sturdy but mobile bridge across the deep ravine, now stoutly anchored at each end. It was almost like a miracle.

The first soldier walked back over the new bridge and carefully touched the lead burro on the nose. The beast began to step after him and the other donkeys behind moved to follow. Each beast stepped gingerly, then firmly on the gently swaying bridge, with one soldier keeping the lead and the second following along behind.

Chico held his breath, his eyes riveted on the bridge, but the donkeys, with their strong instinct for balance, even with blindered eyes and bound-up feet, walked surely and directly across the bridge.

On the opposite side of the ravine, the donkeys were guided in a complete circle and, once again, in the same order, made the precarious crossing back over the little bridge. Just as the lead soldier reached the firm rock on the home side, he glanced up and his face was clear to Chico for the first time. Peering out from under the camouflage helmet was Sergeant Missouri.

"*Bravissimo!*" shouted Chico, leaping to his feet, his heart pounding with excitement, as if he had tried the daring feat himself.

Sergeant Missouri whipped his automatic rifle from the sling on his back and whirled toward Chico with a shout that split the mountain silence. "Halt!" he commanded. "Halt!"

Chico grinned, waved both hands, and then pointed at himself. "Look up here," he said. "It's me, Chico. You know—the friend of Sergeant Donkey!"

The soldier's voice was rough and his rifle was pointed directly at the boy as he spoke. "Keep your hands over your head and march down here on the double," he called.

Chico's heart leaped with a thump of fear. He put his arms up over his head and looked for a way to climb down from the plateau quickly but without falling. Unable to use his hands to hold onto anything for support or his arms for balance, he felt suddenly very awkward and vulnerable. Carefully, he picked his way down the rocks until he stood directly in front of the American sergeant.

"Why are you spying on us?" he demanded, his voice stern.

"I don't spy. I just rest up there," Chico said, trying to point backward with one of the hands still held high.

"What's in that knapsack?" the soldier asked, never shifting the position of his rifle.

"It's filled with honey," Chico told him.

"Turn around," the sergeant ordered gruffly. "I'm tired of your smart answers." Chico turned around obediently and the soldier flipped open the canvas knapsack, ruffled through the green leaves, and then put them back in place.

"What are you doing in the mountains?" the sergeant demanded, his voice still stern.

Chico shrugged and said simply, "I *always* go up the mountains when I go to the abbey. Who else can bring things up to the Brothers? Each week I go, or maybe each two weeks. . . ." Then he explained that the three Brothers were too old and crippled for mountain trails, that the villagers sent them what they could spare themselves and that he, Chico, brought supplies up, and fresh honey down. As he spoke, the soldier swung his rifle back into its casing.

"All right," Sergeant Missouri said, "but don't you realize you could get your head blown off, sneaking up and down the mountains that way?" His voice was brusque but his face was now relaxed and friendly. "Next time you want to make a trip up to the abbey, stop by the Remount Depot first and leave word with me or the major, so we know what's what. It's lucky I saw it was *you* instead of taking a pot shot," the soldier said.

Chico shook his head. His voice was polite but firm. "No, no," he said. "Sergeant Missouri got it wrong. He don't see Chico. First Chico sees *him*."

The sergeant shrugged and patted him on the

shoulder. "Okay, kid. But I'm glad you're still in one piece."

Sergeant Missouri seemed so genuinely concerned that Chico decided it was no time to brag. He remained silent. He did not tell the sergeant that once he had even managed to take medicine up the mountain to ailing Brother Gregorio while the Germans were using the Abbey of San Isidro as a citadel. It had been a chilly night, noisy with wind, and Chico had crept along back trails. No one, not even the German guards at the abbey, had seen him as he slipped the package into Brother Gregorio's bed-cell window and made his way back to the village. No one at all.

*   *   *

For the next few days Chico went to his accustomed place under the fig tree just before dusk to watch the animals. The Remount Depot, from the front offices to the veterinarians' examining stalls, was an area bustling with activity, and the scenes in the paddocks were constantly changing and fascinating. Just as soon as one group of mules or donkeys was sent up to the fighting fronts, farther to the north of Italy, truckloads of replacements arrived at the Depot to be examined, processed, and, if need be, trained for their new work. Many of the fresh animals came by troop boat from the United States. Others were still arriving from North Africa.

In all the comings and goings, only Sergeant Donkey seemed to be left behind, limping still, with his hind leg braced and bandaged. Frequently Chico called out to him and held out bunches of dried grass as a lure. Soon the donkey became friendly enough to limp close to the fence and let Chico rub him gently between the eyes. The boy talked to him softly, soothingly, in Italian, and the little animal stood patient and quiet, seeming to enjoy the gentle, aimless companionship.

One afternoon, a while later, Chico saw Sergeant Missouri moving about the paddock, picking out teams of new animals for mountain training. The American waved to the boy and then walked over to the fence.

"The vet says he's going to take the splints off the little fellow here in about two days. That knee joint should be healed by then." Sergeant Donkey stood beside the soldier, nuzzling at his pocket as he spoke.

"He follows me around like a dog," the young soldier said with a laugh. "He's always after me for a piece of chocolate." He put his hand in his pocket and took out half a chocolate candy bar, still wrapped in silver paper. "Here, Chico, you feed him," he said. "Just watch how he likes it."

Chico took the candy, his hand trembling. Suddenly, his mouth watered and his nose almost twitched at the sweet smell. It was more than two years since the boy had tasted chocolate and he fought back the sharp temptation to pop the candy into his own mouth. Chico felt his heart beat faster, then he stiffened his face with pride. Without a word, he unwrapped the chocolate and placed it on his flattened palm, offering it through the wire to the donkey. The little beast licked it up with his rough tongue and then stood almost motionless, his eyes on Chico, his jaws moving slowly as the chocolate melted in his mouth. Chico forced a small smile. "Sergeant Donkey likes it very much," he said.

"He's a real sweet little devil," the sergeant said fondly. "Smart as they come. I don't know what I'd do without him for company."

Next morning, the winter rains began, steady, gray, and cold. Even with his grandfather's old shepherd's cape, which Annalisa had carefully cut down for him, the weather was too wet and miserable for Chico to sit under the fig tree.

*   *   *

It was near the end of the first week of December when Father Antonio asked Chico to take some things up to the abbey once again. Brother Gregorio suffered from gout and chilblains and in the winter months the cold stone floors of the building were a torture to his swollen feet. The village carpenter had made him a pair of crutches and Father Antonio had somehow found some strips of red flannel to use as bandages. And there were other things to take.

The grocer agreed to donate a small sack of salt; the butcher made good his promise of two stewing rabbits, and Annalisa had insisted that Chico cut two heads of cabbage from their patch, even though the heads were too bulky to fit into his knapsack. By eight in the morning, Chico was ready. With his knapsack on his back, the rough crutches under one arm and a cabbage held in each hand, Chico obediently set off for the Remount Depot to report that he was going up to the mountain.

The two guards at the front gate of the encampment listened to his message and gave him permission to enter. Inside, he crossed the big stone courtyard and stared at the various buildings marked with signs written in English. Feeling shy and out of place, he asked the first soldier he met where he could find Sergeant Missouri.

The man was so tall he had to stoop a little to catch Chico's word. "Step in here," he said, "and I'll buzz the stables. Missouri is generally down there at this hour."

Chico followed him into a small office, crowded with a big desk and chair, filing cabinets, a wall map, and an iron potbellied stove glowing with the heat of a wood fire. The soldier picked up a telephone, pressed a buzzer, and said, "Tell Sergeant Missouri there's someone here to see him." Then he sat down at the desk and began to go through the heap of papers laid out before him. Trying to be as inconspicuous as possible, Chico laid the crutches and cabbage heads down on the floor and leaned back against the wall to wait.

A few moments later, Sergeant Missouri stepped into the room and after a brisk salute and "Thank you, Major," to the man seated at the desk, he turned to Chico.

The boy felt so embarrassed and ill at ease in the strange, warm office that he couldn't think of a word of English to say. He just pointed to the things on the floor and whispered shakily, "San Isidro."

"Good boy! You're going up to the abbey today," Sergeant Missouri said. "And you checked in just like I told you to. Do you want to take a look at Sergeant Donkey while you're here?"

Chico nodded dumbly. He felt he would agree to anything just to get out of the major's office. Sergeant Missouri led the way out the door, along one side of the courtyard, and then down a long alleyway between a double row of stables.

"We've got him out back now, right near the enlisted men's barracks," Sergeant Missouri explained. "The vet took the splints off yesterday and the donkey can walk, no trouble or pain or anything, but he's got a limp. He'll always have that, the vet says. Something just didn't knit right. He's still a good little burro but he has limped himself right out of this war. We just couldn't send out an animal with a gimpy leg."

At that moment the two were walking past an open stall where a soldier was standing beside a

tethered pale-gray African donkey, spraying the beast all over with what looked like brown paint. Chico stopped and stared in amazement.

Sergeant Missouri laughed aloud. "This is the beauty shop. We're giving that donkey a hair-dye treatment, right down to his tail. We do a camouflage job on all the light-colored animals—mules, too. Sometimes they have to pack rations to within a few hundred yards of the enemy. We can't take any chances on using animals that might show up at night. It would be suicide for the men *and* the animals to send a light-colored animal up front. Lots of our pack trains up north have to sneak in after dark.

"A good dye job can last anywhere from one to two months," he added, "depending on whether the weather is wet or dry."

The next row of stables was lined with big gray mules; part of the shipment that had come in from

Missouri, the sergeant explained. At the sound of their footsteps, one mule burst into a loud, raucous heehaw; another mule down the line took up the braying until the two split the air with their hoarse clamor.

"That's another thing we've really got to look out for before shipping animals up north," the sergeant continued. "Some of these babies just can't keep their mouths shut. . . . Those two mules making all the noise will be just fine pulling supply wagons behind the fighting front—but they can't do any work for us where we're trying to *sneak* in. They won't be fit for medicine or ammunition packs. That noise would carry half a mile. The Germans could spot our location in a minute.

"Some mules just seem to be born with the heehaw habit. Back home we call those fellows 'Missouri nightingales,'" the sergeant said and laughed.

Chico laughed, too, even though he didn't quite understand the joke. He laughed partly from the sheer excitement and stimulus of being inside the Remount Depot grounds. After years of wartime poverty, without work animals, these rows and rows of stables, all the stalls filled with sturdy, healthy beasts, seemed like wealth and power beyond imagining.

At the far end of the stables, in a small section by himself, stood Sergeant Donkey. At the sight of Chico, he limped toward the boy and then lifted his soft silver face to be petted.

"See? He remembers you," said the sergeant. "Except for that little limp, he's right as rain."

The boy bent over and rubbed his cheek against the donkey's soft nose. The little beast rubbed back. For a moment, Chico thought he felt tears spring into his eyes. He tried to blink them away quickly. Just to be with animals again was no reason to cry, so he made his voice deliberately steady and bright as he said, "You've got a real good donkey, Sergeant. Real fine. Thank you for letting me . . ."

Sergeant Missouri seemed to be mulling something over in his mind. His tanned, handsome face was thoughtful. "Seems to me this donkey could stand a little exercise," he said. "You planning to hike all the way up to the abbey with those crutches and that stuff you left in the major's office?"

The boy nodded.

"You'd be doing us a favor if you'd take him up the mountain and back. He's still a good pack animal—"

Chico's mouth was suddenly dry with excitement. "*Me* take Sergeant Donkey?" he cried, unbelieving.

"Don't see why not," the sergeant said simply. "Be danged if I can see *why not.*"

A few minutes later, Chico led the burro out the front gate of the encampment, properly geared, and with the cabbage heads in one straw pannier, the crutches for Brother Gregorio sticking out of the other. Outside the gate, he mounted the donkey, his thin brown legs jutting out over the saddle baskets on either side. Holding the reins in his left hand, he looked back at Sergeant Missouri, giving him a smile and a smart salute. Then the donkey and boy trotted off through the thin rain heading toward the mountains. Neither Chico nor the burro seemed bothered or concerned about the small, jerking limp in one hind leg.

*   *   *

In the next few weeks Chico borrowed Sergeant Donkey three more times to make his supply trips to the Abbey of San Isidro. Once Sergeant Missouri added two cans of corned beef to the meager supplies. On another occasion, he sent along a large box of powdered milk. Each time Chico returned the donkey to its stall, he carefully cleaned all the gear, from bridle to panniers, and hung it on hooks on the stable wall. Then he rubbed down the little animal with a rough cloth and curry-combed it briskly until the silver coat was silken smooth. Through it all, the donkey stood quiet, as docile and patient as a pet dog.

Frequently, on other afternoons, Chico stopped by the Remount Depot just to talk to Sergeant Missouri or to lend a hand with whatever chores he might be doing. The bustle and activity of the encampment were in sharp contrast to the cold and emptiness of Chico's own house that winter. With all her efforts, young Annalisa, pale and thin shoulders huddled in an old sweater, could not make a comfortable, busy home without enough food to fill a pot or enough fuel to make a warm fire.

The big sergeant liked to talk during Chico's visits. Sometimes he seemed to chatter on to himself as much as to the boy. And he talked to the mules and donkeys as if he half expected them to nod their heads and join the conversation. It never occurred to Chico that Sergeant Missouri, like a lot of other soldiers, was far from home—and lonely.

The operation of the Remount Depot had added a tone of new life to the sleepy village of San Palio. Often in the evening the little streets, and especially the cafés on the village square, were crowded with soldiers, looking for relaxation. And the coming and going of truckloads of animals, new beasts arriving, trained and fitted animals going out, kept the main road into town filled with loud noise.

"We're doing right good," the sergeant once remarked proudly to Chico. "The major says we're processing animals and shipping them up north at the rate of a thousand a month. That means we've put almost three thousand mules and donkeys into action already. And we've got thousands more ready to be delivered when we get stable room."

It made Chico feel very grown up to be talked to this way and to have a friend as important as the sergeant. One evening, when the weather was especially bitter and the rain cold, the sergeant drove the boy from camp back to San Palio in an army jeep, letting

him off at the corner of his street because the cobblestoned lane was too narrow for the car. As Chico darted through the rain, he noticed two neighbors staring out at Sergeant Missouri. He felt suddenly very proud of the tall, blond stranger who had become his friend.

*   *   *

The holiday season of Christmas comes every year, even in wartime. Chico knew the day was approaching, not by watching the calendar but by the sullen heaviness that filled his heart. He felt a helplessness that was almost painful when he thought of his little brother and sister and the bleak day they would have.

He himself could remember prewar Christmases, with little roast pigs, browned skin crisp and crackling, and fig puddings that steamed on the stove with a warmth and sweetness of odor that filled the whole house. He could remember toy trains and tops to spin on the floor and new red mittens to wear to church, and the bells for Midnight Mass chiming out over a peaceful village. But his young brother and sister had known almost nothing but war. Children always *believed* there would be a good Christmas, Chico felt, and, as man of the house, it seemed so wrong not to keep faith with them.

On the last few days before Christmas, he even avoided the Remount Depot. The home-made wreath of whortleberry that someone had hung at the front gate, the bright American Christmas cards tacked on the walls of the barracks, the glow of potbellied stoves, and the general holiday air of the encampment seemed too removed from the harshness of life in the village. It was too difficult to offer holiday best wishes to those who already had everything for which they could possibly wish.

On Christmas morning, scrubbed clean and in the best clothes they had, Chico, Annalisa, and the two youngest Filippos walked to church for eleven-o'clock Mass. There were not enough candles left in the village to light up the church for Midnight Mass. Father Antonio had cut some fir branches from the mountains to decorate the altar and the tiny, white-walled church was sharp with the scent of pine. In one corner, the traditional manger scene had been set up, with the Three Kings and shepherds in the background, Saint Joseph leaning on a staff, and the Blessed Mother, bending over the crib with sad smile and outstretched arms. A silver paper star, hanging by a string over the manger, shifted and turned in the cold drafts that filled the church and Baby Jesus, in his bed of straw, looked strangely chill and forlorn. Light filtered through the two stained-glass windows on either side of the church, sprinkling the floor with colored patterns whose reflected brightness seemed as cold as the glass itself.

Chico followed the Mass carefully, bowing his head and trying to force his heart to say thank you to the Christ Child who had brought peace on earth and good will toward men. Annalisa, her dark hair covered with a lace mantilla, prayed with motionless intensity, her pale face as lovely as that of a saintly statue.

The boy was somewhat warmed and cheered by the familiar, majestic ritual of the Mass. But as he dipped his fingers into the holy-water font on leaving the church, he felt a thin, fragile skin of ice. Outside, it still rained, but it was almost cold enough to snow.

At home, the little children were given their presents. Annalisa had made Maria, the youngest, a wobbly rag doll, its rounded pink face embroidered into a bright smile. For six-year-old Leonardo, Chico had carved a riding horse—a simple horse's head with painted eyes and mouth and stubby, tacked-on ears made of leather, all mounted on an old broomstick.

Before the little shrine to the Blessed Virgin, in a corner of the front parlor—the same room in which the family ate—Annalisa had lit one precious candle. The light flickered over the bouquet of wax flowers in a vase before the statue, and revealed the gentle, beloved features, crowned with an elaborate tiara of crimped tin and red-glass stones. The excited noise of the two young children and even the glow of one candle gave the room a Christmas brightness, Chico decided.

Annalisa, determined to make the day a special one, made a great, bustling fuss about preparing the Christmas dinner of spaghetti topped with tomato sauce and a sprinkle of dried hot peppers and a salad of cabbage leaves, seasoned with oil and vinegar. His sister had confided in Chico that she had something very special for dessert—four thick slices of bread soaked with honey from Brother Honeycake's hives. Just before serving, she would fry the sweet bread in a little olive oil, until it was toasted as brown and crisp, and hot as a waffle. The little children would be so surprised and delighted!

The family sat down at the table in late afternoon, heads bowed in prayer, while spicy steam rose from the plates of spaghetti, fogging over the windowpanes and giving a mood of warmth to the room. The candle before the Virgin still sputtered and glowed. Chico felt his whole body fill with gratitude as the first taste of tomato sauce and the sharp bite of hot peppers touched his tongue.

Just at that moment there was a knock on the door, a rap so sharp that it shook the old wooden

frame. Chico put down his fork and looked ques-
tioningly at Annalisa. "Who?" he asked. "Father Antonio?" His sister shrugged.

He rose to open the door. There on the front step,
smiling, his blond hair darkened with rain, stood Sergeant Missouri. "I didn't see you round the Depot
for a few days," the sergeant said to Chico, "so I
thought I'd stop by and wish a Merry Christmas to
you and your family. . . ."

The boy paused. He realized this was a social call,
that the sergeant expected to be asked in. So, with a
sweeping gesture of his arm, he said, "Come in! Come
in!" trying desperately to make his voice sound warm
and welcoming.

The sergeant stepped inside, his height and broad
shoulders suddenly making the room seem small and
cramped. "My family," Chico said formally. "My sister, Annalisa, and the little ones, Maria and Leonardo."
The big soldier shook hands with each in turn, bending forward a little at the waist in a stiff, old-fashioned
bow.

"Do take a chair and join us," said Annalisa gra-
ciously, very proud of the English she had learned at
school.

The sergeant hesitated. "We had Christmas dinner at noontime up at the camp," he told her. "I
didn't mean to break in on you this way."

"You are most welcome," Annalisa urged, and Sergeant Missouri slipped off his outside coat, drew a

chair up just a little way from the table, and sat down.

But with his presence, the family conversation became stiff and slow. The little children, awed at having a strange guest at the table, stared at him, dribbling spaghetti sauce on their chins and almost missing their mouths with their forks. It was Annalisa and the sergeant who spoke most—polite little comments about the cold weather, the wind from the mountains, the children's gifts—all interspersed with many smiles and much nodding of heads.

Chico ate quickly and silently, his face stiff with a sudden anger. He did not know why he burned inside with such a fierce resentment toward the sergeant. This was the man who was his friend, the man who had lent him Sergeant Donkey for four separate trips to the abbey. . . . At the Remount Depot, he was exciting, but here, in this house, he simply spoiled their meager holiday. He had come on Christmas Day. He saw how poor they were. He would pity them. Chico realized then that his anger was rooted in helpless shame.

In his mind, he wanted to lash out at the sergeant, to shout at him, "Of course you are big. Of course you are healthy. *Big and healthy like a mule from Missouri.* You eat, you have warm clothes. You are not poor like us. . . ."

Chico did not feel ashamed for his little sister and brother. They were thin and underfed but still they were tiny and pretty, as children so often are. It was toward Annalisa that he felt most defensive. In the sergeant's safe country, girls of nineteen must be big and plump, with strong arms and legs and cheeks pink with health. They would have silk stockings and shoes with heels that clicked. But Annalisa was slim and fragile, her skin as white as a lily petal and her big dark eyes touched underneath with blue shadows. He wanted to tell the sergeant that, in the old days, the days before the war, Annalisa Filippo had been considered one of the most beautiful girls in the village. At fourteen, she had worn a blue dress for her Confirmation in the village church, and the neighbors had said, "Annalisa looks like a queen!"

As Chico's thoughts raged through his own head, his sister and the sergeant chatted stiffly beside him. Finally, the last of the spaghetti was eaten. Annalisa brought fresh plates and served her brothers and sister each a portion of salad. By unspoken agreement, they all ate slowly, making this a festive meal, pretending it was a grand feast that took a long time to eat and enjoy.

Sergeant Missouri took out a package of cigarettes and asked Annalisa's permission to smoke. "But certainly," she said with a smile.

Grudgingly, Chico admitted to himself that the sergeant had very fine manners. He knew how to treat the lady of the house.

After the salad, Annalisa excused herself, explaining that she had something to prepare in the kitchen.

In the silence that followed, Chico tried desperately to think of something pleasant, something natural to say. The sergeant was quiet, puffing on his cigarette. After a while he turned toward Leonardo, pursed his lips, and blew out a tight, blue smoke ring. The ring spread wider as it floated through the air, circling and disappearing almost exactly over the little boy's head.

"Santo Leonardo," the sergeant said. "I gave you a halo." Leonardo looked up and clapped his hands in astonishment.

Then the sergeant blew a series of three quick little smoke rings that went straight for Maria and dissolved just before her eyes. "More," she said in Italian. "Oh, more, please!"

The sergeant lit a fresh cigarette and puffed out smoke ring after smoke ring that circled, twisted, and disappeared over the table top while the children clapped as if they were watching a small circus.

"Now hold out your third finger, left hand," Sergeant Missouri said to Maria.

Chico translated to her and the little girl solemnly did as she was told. The sergeant drew in on the cigarette, then puffed out one fat, careful smoke ring that floated down and encircled itself exactly around the little girl's outstretched finger.

"Now we are engaged to be married," Sergeant Missouri said with a straight face. Chico translated and the little girl laughed and rocked in her chair, hugging her hand to her chest.

At that moment, Annalisa came out of the kitchen with a tray holding five saucers of Christmas cake, the fried honey bread. Her own portion had been carefully cut in half to share with their guest.

He looked at his plate with what seemed genuine delight. "Well, thank you, ma'am," he said warmly. "This is a treat I didn't expect." He smiled at Annalisa. The girl smoothed a hand over her soft, dark hair and her cheeks were faintly pink.

Chico felt his own heart soften at the soldier's

simple words. Sergeant Missouri was behaving with gallantry. He did not dishonor the house.

After the last crumb of honey-sweet bread had been eaten, Sergeant Missouri looked at his wrist watch and said, "I've got an hour or more before I have to check in at camp. I'd appreciate it, Chico, if you'd show me around your farm."

"But it's not a farm *now*," Chico protested. "It's just emptiness and idle fields with no tools, no people. . . ."

The sergeant nodded and said quietly, "I know that. But I farm back home in Missouri, with my father and older brother. It would just seem more like home to me, more like it was Christmas, if I had a chance to see your farm."

The sergeant put on his heavy coat, while Chico went to fetch his own cut-down shepherd's cape. Then the two stepped out into the light, chill drizzle of rain.

First Chico took the sergeant behind the house, pointing out the door to the root cellar and the open pens that had held the sheep and goats when they were not out to pasture. Then he showed him the shed, half roofless now, that had housed the two donkeys. In the corner of the shed was a rusting plow, a digging fork and spade, and an old wheelbarrow with no front wheel. "All is different before the war, when my father is here," Chico explained. "Now I am a bad farmer. I have almost no crops. I have no animals, no good tools. . . ."

"I know," said the sergeant. "There just is so much a man can do with his own two hands."

Together they trudged down the village street and out into the open countryside where the six fields of Chico's father lay side by side, carefully marked off by low stone fences.

In spite of his hot, early anger, Chico now found himself pointing things out talking, and explaining. The sergeant's mood and the expression on his face were solemn and attentive, as if this tour of the small acreage was a very serious thing to him. His father had planted no grains, Chico explained. Rather, he had specialized in vegetables—tomatoes, peppers, squashes—the kinds of food a village housewife might expect to buy fresh in the market each day. And every spring, his father had planted two whole fields with honeydew melons. Mr. Filippo was famous for his good melons, Chico rattled on—small melons, light yellow-green and smooth-skinned, almost perfectly round, superbly sweet and soft inside. At the height of the fall harvest season, his father had hired two extra men from the village as pickers and a small truckload of Filippo melons was rushed up to Naples each day.

The sergeant squatted down and rubbed some damp, black soil thoughtfully between his fingers. "Looks like good earth you've got here," he said.

"God gives us good soil, good rain, and good sun—and we do the work," Chico said with a laugh, quoting an old proverb. "Until the war," he added sadly.

When the two friends were back at the little house in the village once more, Sergeant Missouri paused on the front doorstep and said hesitantly, "I'd like to say good-by to your sister and thank her, if you don't mind."

Chico opened the door. Inside, the front room was still and orderly, the table cleared, the chairs lined back against the wall. Maria and Leonardo played quietly on an old blanket spread on the cold marble floor. Annalisa sat sewing on a chair near the window, shadowy and fragile in the failing light of evening.

"I wanted to thank you, ma'am," said Sergeant Missouri.

Annalisa smiled and nodded.

He paused, looked around the room for a moment, and then stepped over to the little table holding the bowl of wax flowers and the statue of the Blessed Virgin. The single candle had long since burned down and guttered out.

"I know how most women feel about kids eating between meals," he said gravely to Annalisa, "so I'll just put these right here and maybe you can give some to the children when you think the time is right." Out of his coat pocket he pulled eight chocolate bars and piled them neatly on the table before the statue.

"Many thanks," whispered Annalisa, her great eyes luminous in the dark room.

Sergeant Missouri gave her a smile and a soft salute, touching his fingers to his forehead. "Merry Christmas to you all," he said. Then he turned back to the shrine. "Merry Christmas," he said again, as if the statue were alive and equally deserving of courtesies.

After he left, Annalisa finished the pair of socks she was darning, working neatly and slowly, and snapped off the last thread with her fine white teeth.

"I like your big friend, Chico," she said simply. "And I think *now* is the time for us all to have some Christmas candy."

*   *   *

After that first visit, Sergeant Missouri went to see the Filippo family again and again. By the end of January, his visits were quite regular, usually every Sunday afternoon, just at dusk. He and Chico sat in the front room, talking as men do, and Annalisa always joined them for an hour or so. Twice Sergeant Missouri asked Annalisa if she would care to walk to the village café with him for a glass of wine. Chico felt his friend was most thoughtful. His sister was at home so much with the children, she needed a change of scene.

Both times he fell asleep in his little bedroom before the two arrived back home but the sounds of their murmuring voices from the front room waked him. Drowsily, he fell off to sleep again, wondering what they could possibly find to talk about. But he felt proud of Annalisa. He had not realized she knew so much English.

Through the long, gray, wet days of that winter, the Remount Depot worked with doubled intensity. For the Americans, the war news from the north of Italy—and from Europe—was frequently very bad. Fighting was bitter and intense. Often troops had to capture, lose, and then fight to retake the same few miles of land. At the Depot, the mood was sometimes grim, the men tired and discouraged. Along with fresh animals for processing, numbers of mules and donkeys were sent back from the fighting front, wounded and in need of medical care, like any disabled soldier. There was not an empty stall—nor a pair of idle hands—in the whole encampment.

*   *   *

On one mid-March afternoon, Sergeant Missouri and Private Tommy Mazur were trail-breaking a string of mules in the area below the abbey. Except for the lead animal, the mules were fresh recruits—and so was Tommy Mazur. They were just off the Stateside boat, and unaccustomed to the rocky paths that twisted in serpentine loops through the heavy underbrush and thick stands of pines.

In the States, these farm mules were accustomed to pulling plows or wagons in double-harness teams. Now they were being put through the routine of walking narrow trails in single file, with loaded packs, following faithfully after the well-trained lead mule. Sergeant Missouri, at the head of the string of eight, turned and called back to Tommy Mazur, "Keep 'em close together. Keep 'em moving."

An hour ago, farther back on the trail, young Mazur had twisted his ankle badly on a mossy rock and now he was riding back to camp astride the last mule, his swollen, injured foot resting on one of the saddlebags as he held the reins lightly in his hand.

It had been a rainless day, but damply chill. Long lances of sunshine broke through the green limbs above their heads, coating the hard, uneven trails with a pale golden light. But Sergeant Missouri could feel the moist, cold wind against his face and he knew it would be a night of fog and mists in the valley ahead.

"Keep 'em moving," he yelled, tugging hard on the reins of the lead mule. The Remount Depot was still an hour's march away, and Sergeant Missouri hoped to have Mazur in the infirmary and his mules stabled before dark.

"Hold it, Sarge," Tommy Mazur called to him, and when Sergeant Missouri turned and looked over his shoulder, he saw that the young soldier had reined in his mule and was frowning at a shelf of rock which towered above that part of the trail like a rough platform.

The shifting lights played across Private Mazur's face, and he raised his hand to his eyes to shield them from the glare.

"What is it?" Sergeant Missouri called to him.

"Thought I heard something."

It was at that instant, as Tommy searched the tall, flat cropping of rock with troubled eyes, that a shot rang out with shocking abruptness and, whistled sharply past his head, the echoes banging and hissing spitefully down the valley. Private Mazur threw himself forward, face downward, arms hugging tightly around the mule's thick neck. Another shot sounded, ricocheting wildly through the trees. Missouri released his hold on the bridle of the lead mule and gave the animal a sharp slap on the flank with his hand. "Back to camp, git!" he shouted at the animal. The veteran mule set off down the familiar path in a frenzied dash, the other seven mules clattering close behind. For a brief moment, Missouri watched Mazur bounced and jostled, until the young soldier got a solid grip on the frightened rear mule he rode. The attack was so unexpected that the sergeant had barely had time to think and no time to run. Already, the clatter of the mule team was fading as the animals dashed down the mountainside toward the valley and safety.

Sergeant Missouri threw himself behind a tree,

peering around it for a view of the shelf of rock thirty yards above his head. Cautiously, Missouri unslung his rifle and pumped off three rounds at the face of the ledge of rock, the bullets sending fragments of stone whining through the air. Scrambling sideways toward a heavy boulder, he saw a soldier's helmet appear among the rocks, above him. Missouri had only a glimpse of the soldier's face, but he knew it was an enemy. The low, curving sides of the helmet told him that instantly.

A shot sounded before Missouri could pull himself behind the heavy cropping of rock, and there was a stab of pain in his left thigh, a hot needle driving into his flesh. He didn't know how bad it was. There was only the pain now, and the blood beginning to stain his gray-green fatigue trousers.

He drew a deep breath and lay motionless behind the protecting rock. Above him, he heard voices speaking in German, the heavy, guttural sounds falling clear through the fading light.

Missouri made himself lie still. It wasn't easy. His impulse was to move out, to try to scramble down the trail after the mules. But he knew this would just make the enemies' job easier. In the open they'd gun him down like a bird with a broken wing. No, if they wanted him, they could come and get him.

He wondered why they were waiting. The talking had stopped. There was no sound at all, except the light wind rustling branches high above his head. His foe had all the cards—superior fire power, superior numbers, superior positions. Why were they hesitating? It could be, he thought, the Germans didn't know exactly what they were up against. And Missouri decided it would be real good if they were kept in doubt about that . . . for as long as possible. . . .

He squirmed to a sitting position, grunting against the pain, and snapped two shots at the face of the cliff. Before the echoes faded, he had scrambled sideways to crouch behind the trunk of a fallen tree. It was darker now, but there were still dangerous reflections of sunlight flickering along the trail.

Missouri fired again, moved again, fired again, moved again—and then he stopped and shouted, "Johnny! Mike! All you men! Hold your fire. No more shooting."

It might buy him some time, he thought, might worry them a little. They might figure they had a detail or even a patrol pinned down, instead of a beat-up, mule-skinning sergeant with a bullet hole in his leg. Missouri listened for sounds, while he prayed for the darkness to cover him like a great big blanket. He eased back the bolt of his rifle, slipped a fresh clip of ammunition into the breach, and let a round slide slowly into the chamber, with no telltale click, no revealing whisper of brass on steel.

To his left and right, the narrow trail stretched away into deepening shadows. To try to crawl up toward the abbey, or down toward the Depot—either way the path was directly below the Germans. An empty silent pathway through the forests—but a path that would be suicide to use.

Missouri backed slowly, quietly away from the trail, dragging himself like a crab through thorny under-brush, across stretches of rock that cut and ripped at his uniform like broken razor blades. Finally, out of sight and sound of the Germans, he pulled the walkie-talkie from the leather case attached to his cartridge belt, and switched on the Remount Depot's channel.

"Red Dog One," he said, so softly that only a wisp of his breath showed white against the chill air. "Sergeant Missouri to Red Dog One. Over."

There was a click in his ears, then the Depot dispatcher's casual voice. "Red Dog One to Sergeant Missouri. Over."

Missouri gave it to him quickly. "We got hit by Germans. Mazur's headed back toward the Depot on a runaway mule. He's got a bad ankle but that lead jenny mule should run the whole string right into camp. I'm pinned down near that rock shelf, half-mile or so from the abbey, with a bullet in my leg."

Missouri slipped off his belt and looped it around his thigh, buckling it as tightly as possible. To make the tourniquet more effective, he needed a slim, strong piece of wood to slip under the belt, turning it to increase the pressure. But he decided against that. The noise he made trying to find the wood could be just as fatal as loss of blood or an infected wound.

The major's voice sounded tensely in his ear. "Sergeant Missouri, how badly are you hit? Can you move out?"

"It's in my leg, I don't know how bad, sir. I could crawl, but not fast and not far. And they've got the path covered."

"Now listen to me. We had an alert from Intelligence an hour ago. A German patrol is heading south. They got through our lines. May be a reconnaissance group. Or out to take prisoners. Intelligence doesn't know. But all ground troops are on maximum alert. Nobody thought they could get this far, though. We haven't had a German patrol in this area for months. Now, how many German soldiers have you seen?"

"Just one, sir. But there might be a half-dozen, judging from the firing and the voices."

"We can call Naples for P-47 planes. Give me your position, as exact as you can make it."

"My grid coordinates are about—well, I'd say, numeral B for Baker. It's where the big rock ledge hangs out over the main trail from the abbey. I'm off trail in the brush now, to the right coming up from the Depot. There're two big fallen trees here, lying in a kind of crisscross. But one thing, Major. I set loose my string of mules."

"Don't worry about that."

"I just don't want any fly-boys machine-gunning those mules, with Tommy Mazur aboard, sir."

The major spoke briskly. "Okay, just you hang on, Missouri. We'll do our darnedest to get you out of there."

The connection was broken, with a dry click of finality.

Sergeant Missouri crouched close to the ground, pulling up his collar against the bitter, gusting winds. Show me, he thought tiredly, I'm from Missouri.

High above him, patient and impregnable, were the Germans, Missouri knew, watching the trail for the slightest movement, listening for the crack of a twig, the rattle of rocks. . . .

Soon they'd be coming for him. Probably in the first light of morning. The sergeant made sure his rifle was off safe. Then he settled down to wait, trying not to think of the pain in his leg.

*   *   *

In the Remount Depot's communications room there was no sound but the crackle of wood burning in the potbellied stove, the occasional distant braying of stabled animals. No one was talking. The dispatcher sat at the radio desk, occasionally flicking a worried glance at Major Desmond and Captain Anderson, who were studying the small-scale map of the mountains immediately above the Depot.

Captain Anderson, a stocky blond man, with cool, level eyes, looked at the major and said, "Well, the

Air Force promises us P-47's. That's something."
There was a distinctly cheerless note in his voice.

The major nodded bitterly. "Of course, at dawn.
They can't do anything now but scare livestock."

The stove belched smoke as the door was pushed
open, and Chico slipped into the room. He looked up
at the American officers, his eyes wide and anxious.

"I heard men talk," he said, the words tumbling
out so rapidly that they blurred together into a single liquid murmur. "Sergeant Missouri hurt."

"Yes," the major told him quietly. "He's hurt, Chico.
There's a German patrol up there."

"Where is Sergeant Missouri?"

Major Desmond took a pencil from his pocket
and pointed to the intersections of grid lines Four
and B. "Just about here. There's a big ledge of rock
over the trail. The Germans are there. Missouri's off-
trail in the woods—about there." He pointed again.

"You go get him now?" Chico asked anxiously.

Something in the major's troubled expression caused
a knot of fear to tighten in the boy's stomach. He
looked at the captain and saw the same worried expression on the younger officer's face. It was a strange
and frightening moment to Chico, for he had never
before seen Americans when they were helpless.

"We can't go and get him," the major explained
quietly. "Not while a German patrol is covering the
trail. I can send men to die, but not to commit
suicide."

"But Sergeant Missouri is hurt. He die."

The major turned from the map and rubbed a hand across his forehead. "You'd better go home, Chico."

Chico stared up at him imploringly. "I get him. I go get Sergeant Missouri."

The major shook his head slowly. "You're going home."

Chico turned and looked helplessly at the map. "Show me where you say is the abbey and where you say is Sergeant Missouri. Please show me—*please!*"

The major flicked a puzzled glance at the captain, then circled with his pencil the location of the abbey, pointed to marked paths leading up to it and then traced down one of the marked trails to a second spot. "Here, Chico. About a half-mile to three-quarters of a mile, that's where the sergeant's pinned down. Says he's near a couple of big trees fallen crisscross."

Chico's face suddenly blazed with excitement and impulsively he took the pencil from the major's hand. "You all wrong here, sir. You point out only *old* trails. Chico knows another way. New way." He began tracing on the big map with the eraser end of the pencil. His voice was tense, almost a whisper.

"Look," he said. "Chico goes up to the abbey, not on front path, not near Germans, but through woods and then climb up from behind, up the big rocks. Then I come *down* path to near where Germans are and *back* into woods to get Sergeant Missouri. . . .

Germans watch on big paths for someone coming up. No one will watch for someone coming down. I know exact spot where hides Sergeant Missouri. . . ." In his excitement, Chico's speech slurred into half Italian.

"There aren't any trails at all where you're pointing," said the captain. "Remember, we fought our way up that mountain to capture it in the first place. That area directly behind the abbey is almost sheer cliff. No one could climb it."

Chico shook his head stubbornly, his face determined. "Goats climb it, sheep climb. And once before, just last year, Chico climbed it!"

The major patted the boy's thin shoulders. "I think you'd try it," he said quietly. "I honestly think you would. But it's no good."

"What's no good?"

"It won't work. You couldn't make it alone. And you couldn't bring Missouri down, even if you got to him."

"I don't go alone!" Chico cried desperately. "I go with Sergeant Donkey."

The captain started to shake his head. Then he turned and frowned at the map. The silence became charged with tension. After a moment, the major looked thoughtfully at Captain Anderson.

"No," the captain said, with a vigorous headshake, "no, Major. That is, if you intend to ask my advice."

"I don't," Major Desmond said drily. "No point in both of us standing trial before a court-martial."

He caught Chico's shoulders in his big hands and looked steadily, directly into the boy's eyes.

"Now listen," he said quietly. "You know a second trail that leads to where the sergeant's pinned down? Another way to go?"

Chico nodded slowly, but with assurance.

"Okay," the major said. "You can get to him from the abbey? You know a way? You're sure?"

Again, Chico nodded slowly and firmly. "I can make trip with Sergeant Donkey. In his saddlebags you put us food and medicine for Sergeant Missouri. . . ."

Major Desmond smiled faintly and shook Chico's shoulders gently. "That's not all we'll put in those saddlebags." He glanced sharply at Captain Anderson. "Ring the supply sergeant. Tell him to report to the supply room—on the double."

Turning to the radio dispatcher, he said, "Call Missouri. Tell him we're going to try to get help up to him tonight."

*   *   *

Astride the little burro, the trip across the valley was rapid and wordless for Chico. It was only when he came to the first foothills of the mountain and reined his mount sharply off to the right, away from the open paths, that he whispered, "Now, Sergeant Donkey. Now we begin."

Slowly, with the burro picking his way along on almost soundless feet, Chico guided him in a zigzagging course up and around the side of the mountain, weaving among trees and covering pathless ground that was blanketed with pine needles. It was a misty night, with swirls of fog over the valley and small wisps hanging here and there among the trees. It took more than an hour for the boy and the donkey to wind up and out of the mountain forest and stand at the bottom of the great cliff that backed the abbey.

Here Chico slipped off the burro's back, silent and thoughtful, trying to peer through the mists up the sheer rise of rock. As best he could, the boy racked his memory to recall the twists and turns of the narrow upward trail. Then he took off his sandals, knotted the strings, and slung them around his neck. "Tonight," he told himself wryly, "Chico will think with his feet."

Then he tightened the straps holding the donkey's heavy saddlebags and patted the beast affectionately on the nose. "The trick, little friend," he whispered, "is to go slow. Don't think *up* and don't think *down*. Just go slow. One step at a time."

He held the burro by a short rein, so short that the animal's warm breath was soft on his hand, and the pair began the torturous climb upward, boy leading, donkey stepping carefully behind. Even though his eyes were accustomed to the dark, Chico found the rise and swirl of mists confusing. With one hand he felt along the mountain wall, leaning as closely as he could to the massive rise of rock. On the narrow path, the stones were rough and cold under his bare feet. Because the climb was steep, he felt his breath coming short. Several times he stopped to rest, breathing in deeply to fill his lungs and push out a tight anxiety that had begun to cramp his chest. Each time he paused, the donkey stood patiently behind him.

About halfway up the cliff, the weather began to change. Chico broke through the scattered, foggy mists that had layered the valley and lower mountain. He seemed, suddenly, to come into open air, lit by thin moonlight. Now that the path along the face of the cliff was clearer, its steep narrowness was more terrifying. The boy's pounding heart made him walk more slowly. It was not the altitude that bothered him but a smothering, helpless fear. Alone, on the chill, steep side of the mountain, all the bravery he had felt in the major's warm, bright office began to disappear. He realized that his feet were very bruised and sore from the rocky path and his fingers and knuckles scraped raw from trying to cling to the sharp rocks. His own ragged breathing was a fearful sound in his ears.

At one moment, as Sergeant Donkey struggled for a foothold, a rock was knocked loose and fell tumbling and rattling down the mountainside . . . a long, clattering fall that echoed and re-echoed in the night.

Chico knew then why this journey was so different from the one when he had brought medicine up to Brother Gregorio. That night had been windy, gusts that tossed the treetops and went singing between the rocks. It had been a noisy night, with a wind-swept mountainside that provided a natural cover-up for the climb. But tonight was oddly silent. The entire mountain seemed to be without wind or movement . . . just a still, eerie stretch of night, muffled in total silence. But to worried Chico, it was like a waiting, listening silence.

At last, at the very top of the old goats' trail, the boy and the burro stepped through a gap in the abbey wall, a hole blown through by a German mortar many months before.

Moonlight, not bright but rather shifting and ethereal, touched the old cobblestoned courtyard and the buildings of the abbey, making them seem dreamlike and unreal. Chico bent down to slip on his sandals,

his bruised feet smarting with pain as he tied the strings. From the saddlebags he took strips of heavy cloth and carefully bound Sergeant Donkey's hoofs to make them even more silent on the path ahead. Then he looked at his companion in this risky mission. The little beast stood sturdy and willing as ever, but the thin moonlight seemed to pick him out, silvered, like a coin shining in water. His light coat appeared almost to shimmer in the dim light. Chico slipped off his dark shepherd's cape and draped it over the donkey, camouflaging as much as possible the glistening hide. The night air was cold on the boy's shoulders and he realized that his forehead, his hands, his whole body were damp with the anxiety of pure fear.

The last time he had slipped up the mountainside, evading the Germans, he was only a little Italian, bringing medicine to an ailing monk. Tonight was very different. He had chosen sides. He was with the Americans.

Carefully, he picked his way across the courtyard until he came to Brother Honeycake's bedroom cell, the small window laced over with iron grillwork. "Brother Honeycake," he whispered. "Brother Honeycake. It's Chico!"

Inside, he heard a stir, then a more rapid movement, and shortly Brother Honeycake stepped out into the courtyard. His white hair was standing up wispy and tousled from sleep. His brown monk's habit was wrapped clumsily around his body like an old bathrobe.

In a harsh whisper, coming from a throat dry with apprehension, Chico told the old monk why he had climbed the mountain and what he must do. The Brother nodded. Then Chico said softly, "Brother Honeycake, you must pray for me. The other time, it was a night of noise. I was not afraid. Tonight, Chico is very afraid. . . ."

In the half-darkness, the elderly man stood thinking. . . . Then he squared his shoulders and tied the belt of his habit together in a resolute knot. "Chicito, I will pray for you," he said firmly. "I will pray for you in the chapel. When you *hear* me praying, you are safe to go." And he scurried across the courtyard toward the chapel.

Chico waited, hearing nothing but the beat of his heart and his own tense breathing. Then, suddenly, bursting out in a volume of beauty that shattered the stillness of the night, the boy heard the sound of music, loud, rolling, swelling chords that seemed to fill the whole mountaintop. Brother Honeycake was playing the organ. Since one side of the old chapel had been bombed away and stood open to the air, the organ music became one with the night outside.

Chico felt a smile touch his tense lips as he moved forward to the front gate, with Sergeant Donkey close behind him. Brother Honeycake was saying his prayers to music, music that drowned out every other sound in the night.

Chico and the donkey moved swiftly out the gate and down the main path, but only for a dozen yards. Then the boy led the animal into the woods, following the trail on down the mountainside but at a hidden distance from the path itself. Chico tracked his progress by watching the sky. To his left, where the tops of the trees were open enough to show the moon-touched clouds above, that was the path. Brother Honeycake's music, although fainter now, was still loud enough to cover the sounds made by a snapped twig or the rustle as Sergeant Donkey pushed through underbrush.

When the pair were only a few hundred yards from the flat rock on which the Germans lay hidden, Chico slowed to an almost motionless creeping, covering the ground furtively, one step at a time. Minutes stretched into longer minutes but he did not hurry the pace.

He knew that not far ahead lay the two giant pines, struck down by lightning some years ago and fallen in a crisscross. Finally, he sighted those trees and, as he crept closer, saw the huddle of a body, half hidden in their shadow.

"We are here, Sergeant Missouri," he whispered in a voice trembling with relief. "We have brought you everything."

*   *   *

Missouri twisted about quickly, the muzzle of his rifle pointed toward the sound of the whispered words. Relief flooded through him as he recognized the silhouette of the boy and the donkey against the heavier blackness of trees and brush.

"No talking," the sergeant said, keeping his own voice steady with a conscious physical effort. The wound in his leg, numbed by the cold, had exploded with pain at his sudden turn toward the boy. Chico moved closer, tethered the burro to a fallen tree, and unstrapped the saddlebags. He laid them on the ground beside the sergeant. The big soldier put his arm about the boy's shoulders and pulled him close for warmth.

"You're cold as a skinned cat," he said. "Can you hold on till morning?"

Chico nodded and then reached up to slip his cape off Sergeant Donkey.

*   *   *

The first streaks of dawn probed the blackness above the trees like pale, slender fingers. Chico stirred from a chill half-sleep and rubbed his numbed hands over his face. Nearby stood the little burro who had waited through the long night's vigil like a figure carved of ash-white marble. Sergeant Missouri was a few yards away, silent and crouched low.

The soldier was peering alertly through the dusky light, his eyes roving back and forth across the shelf of rock high above his head. He could see nothing yet, make out no details. The ridge was still concealed by shifting black shadows.

Chico crawled close to him and whispered, "Time *now* that we go?"

Missouri shook his head, without taking his eyes from the ledge of rock. He squinted intently through the layers of dangerously growing light, his ears strained for any human sound—the scrape of boots on the ground, the betraying click of a rifle bolt.

Sergeant Missouri was ready. In the cold, dark hours since Chico's arrival, he had drunk all of the hot, sweet coffee from two thermoses. The strong warmth had spread slowly through his numb, cramped body, even easing the pain in his leg.

While Chico dozed, Missouri had treated his wound with sulfa, strapping it securely with antiseptic gauze and heavy bandages. Miraculously, it seemed to be a clean hit. The bullet had gone through the muscle of his thigh without striking bone. It gave him pain, but he could move.

Last of all, Missouri removed four hand grenades from the saddlebags and placed them in an even row on the ground, close to his right hand. They were aligned in a functional pattern, the firing pins facing the sergeant, the detachable handles facing in the opposite direction. He could pick them up without even having to look at them, and slip a finger into the metal loop attached to the firing pin. The cocking of his right arm would pull the pin, and that was the point of no return. The instant he relaxed his grip on the grenade, the handle would fly off, activating the timing trigger. Five seconds later, the grenade would explode, shattering the air with shrapnel. The big sergeant had four chances—and he was ready.

A rock rattled somewhere on the ledge above the path. Missouri pulled Chico close and whispered sharply into his ear, "Move out—*now*. Take the donkey and get back about thirty yards into the trees. Wait for me. If I'm not there in ten minutes, well— head back to camp, on the double. *Don't come back to look for me.*"

Chico nodded slowly, helplessly.

"Okay then," Missouri said, and gave the boy a hard little smile. "Move out."

"Okay, sir," Chico said, and his voice was suddenly as hard and resolute as Sergeant Missouri's.

At that moment, something stirred on the shelf of rock. Then a probing ray of sunlight broke brilliantly and briefly on a metallic surface—a helmet, a belt buckle, a rifle barrel—Missouri wasn't sure what. He looked quickly after Chico, who was leading the donkey off through the brush, farther away from the trail. Hurry, hurry, boy, he thought, the words forming in his mind like a prayer. Hurry, keep moving. . . .

The metallic snap of a rifle bolt shattered the silence. Missouri focused his attention tensely on the high ledge. Another rifle bolt broke the silence. They were ready now, Missouri realized—no more cat and mouse, no more crouching in the dark, waiting for a shot at him. The sunlight was beginning to come through the trees in golden layers, and the Germans were set to follow it down the hill.

He looked over his shoulder again quickly, just once more, and saw with relief that Chico and the donkey were out of sight, completely hidden in the deeper underbrush. That meant they were out of range. . . .

Suddenly, high above him, a German soldier leaped into full view on the shelf of rock, his face hard and

pale under his gray-green helmet, the rifle at his
shoulder swinging back and forth to cover the ground
and path below the rock. He shouted an order and
two soldiers appeared beside him, rifle butts locked
tightly to their shoulders.

Without taking his eyes from them, Missouri
picked up a grenade. He brought it to his chest,
hooked his left index finger through the loop of the
firing pin, and waited, his narrowing eyes sweeping
back and forth across the three soldiers. One of
them slowly raised a hand in the air, about to order
a cautious descent of the sloping rock while—along
the length of the shelf of rock—five more soldiers
appeared, rising slowly and carefully, their rifles trained
on the ground beneath them.

Missouri swept his right arm back in a full arc,
snapping the pin from the grenade. The movement
caught the eye of the lead German soldier, who
shouted triumphantly and fired a burst at the American soldier. The shots struck the tree beside him,
spraying his cheek with fragments of splintered wood.

"*Auf Wiedersehen,*" Missouri said grimly, and let
the grenade fly, arching it high in the air with a stiff
swing of his right arm. There was a shout high above
him, as the grenade lofted into view, then a pound
of retreating boots, a clatter of falling rocks, as the
grenade landed on the shelf.

Missouri lay flat on the ground, arms locked about
his head.

The explosion shook the air into tatters. Shrapnel whined about his ears, ripping through the trees and underbrush with spiteful, singing sounds. Missouri twisted to a sitting position, and hurled two more grenades farther back onto the shelf of rock, demolishing it completely and cutting off any possible descent of the enemy to the trail below. The echoes of the dual explosions chased the first blast through mountain ravines and gullies in crescendoing patterns of rampaging sound.

Sergeant Missouri waited until the last reverberations had died away. From the ledge of rock no sound came, no movement, just a thin haze of smoke. Cautiously, Missouri pulled himself into a standing position, leaning for support against a tree, lobbed the last grenade through the air, and turned swiftly to hobble into the woods. Crouched in the underbrush, Chico heard him coming and crept forward, leading the burro.

"March order, Chico. March order," Sergeant Missouri gasped and threw himself across the back of the donkey.

Within minutes the three friends were on the main trail, moving swiftly and surely toward safety. Just as they came out on the open fields of the valley, the morning air was split with the staccato thunder of engines. Looking up, Missouri saw a formation of low-flying P-47's on the horizon, heading up the coast from Naples. In spite of his exhaustion and the sharp pain in his thigh, Sergeant Missouri laughed aloud. "They're sending us the Air Force, Chico, and we made it with a donkey," he said.

*   *   *

Spring came early that year. By the end of April, the valley of San Palio lay under clear, warm skies, fields were green, and even the grenade scars on the mountainside had begun to heal over with new growth.

At the Remount Depot, Major Desmond was sitting at his desk, attempting to get his paper work out of the way before the very special ceremony of this particular spring Saturday. Yellow sunlight fell in smooth bars across his desk, coating its surface with a pale liquid sheen and glinting on the thick white coffee mug beside his elbow.

From outside, he could hear the tramp of marching feet and the crisply shouted commands of corporals and sergeants.

The door opened and Captain Anderson came in, saluted, and announced, "The company is assembled, sir."

As the major stood up, Captain Anderson handed him a long envelope and a slim blue box, the cover of which was stamped with gold lettering. Nodding at the envelope, the captain said, "I hope that's in order, sir."

The major smiled briefly and said, "I hope so, too." With the captain at his heels, the major strode from his office and out into the old cobblestone courtyard.

Company A of the Animal Remount Service, one hundred and fifty men strong, including Sergeant Missouri and Private Mazur, was lined up in three rows, facing the major's office. Sunlight shone on sparkling brass, gleaming rifles, and freshly shaven faces. Behind the soldiers, a row of ancient almond trees lined one wall of the courtyard. They were pink with bloom, scenting the spring air.

At one side, near the old stone well, stood a group of civilians—Father Antonio, in full Sunday cassock and three-cornered biretta; Giuseppi Testa, the acting mayor of San Palio, a stoopshouldered old man leaning on a cane; and Annalisa Filippo, her eyes bright and her cheeks as pink as the almond blossoms. Beside her stood Chico, holding Sergeant Donkey by the bridle.

At the stables that morning, someone had curried the donkey until his coat shone and then outfitted the little animal in full gear, from saddle to bridle and panniers. Just before the major came out of his office, a soldier had led the donkey from the stables and given him to Chico to hold.

Father Antonio stood close by the boy, a hand on his shoulder, watching the soldiers with solemn interest. Chico looked at the donkey and then up at the priest. He started to speak, but Father Antonio quickly put a finger to his lips. "We are guests, Chico," he whispered.

At the sight of the major, the company of soldiers came to attention as one man, shoulders squared, eyes staring straight ahead, heels coming together with a booted crack on the cobblestones. The first sergeant eyed them with satisfaction, then wheeled about and saluted the major.

"Company A all present and accounted for, sir."

The major returned the salute, and ordered, "Sergeant, take your post."

When the sergeant reached his position at the head of the column, the major said, "Sergeant John Price, front and center."

Sergeant Missouri moved out from the ranks, his handsome face solemn, his shoulders squared. Only a slight limp in his left leg betrayed the bullet wound that had hospitalized him for nearly six weeks. Coming to attention before the major, he saluted briskly.

The major said, "Sergeant Missouri, I wish we could do this with a full division parade, but there's still a war on. I want you to know, however, that I think you did a fine job, a brave job on the mountain that night." He hesitated a moment, then added with a smile, "And so does the general."

He opened the lid of the slim blue box he was holding, removed a shining silver star, and pinned it to the left breast of Sergeant Missouri's tunic, which already held the Purple Heart medal.

"The Silver Star," Major Desmond said quietly. "You earned it, son, every bit of it, especially for the valor and unselfish thinking that saved the life of Private Thomas Mazur."

Sergeant Missouri had to clear his throat before he could manage to say, "Thank you, sir." He shook hands with the major, turned, and marched back to his position in the ranks, proudly trying to keep any trace of limp out of his rhythmic, swinging stride.

The major looked down at the long, sealed envelope in his hand, then he raised his head, smiled faintly, and said, "Sergeant Donkey—front and center."

Chico's eyes widened with surprise. He looked helplessly, first at Annalisa and then at Father Antonio. The priest nudged him forward, saying, "The burro is wanted. Go on—"

Smiling uncertainly, Chico led Sergeant Donkey across the courtyard, before the triple row of soldiers, and pulled him to a halt in front of Major Desmond.

The major opened the envelope, removed a piece of paper from it, and, after a grave look at Chico's anxious face, cleared his throat and said, "Sergeant Donkey, by the powers invested in me as senior officer of this Remount Depot, I am hereby honorably discharging you from the United States Army. As a reward for your heroic and faithful services, I am" —the major smiled down at the boy—"consigning you without reservation or qualification to the custody of Chico Filippo as his personal donkey."

Chico's eyes lit up like candles. His heart pounded with hope . . . but he just wasn't sure if he under-

stood what all the big words meant. "*Me?*" he asked breathlessly.

"That's right, Chico," the major answered. "He's all yours now. And this paper will explain to anyone who's interested just how you earned him."

He returned the document to the envelope and gave it to Chico, who simply stared at it, as if he held something unreal in his small brown hand.

"I wish I could give you a medal, too," the major said.

"No, no! Sergeant Donkey's all I want," Chico cried eagerly.

"He's all yours then," the major assured him. Turning to the first sergeant, he ordered, "Sergeant, dismiss the company."

On order, the soldiers broke ranks and walked

back to their barracks. They would now change from garrison uniforms into fatigue work clothes and return to their duties, for there was still a war on and thousands of fighting soldiers were waiting for the Remount Division's animal troops.

Chico led Sergeant Donkey back to where the priest, the mayor, and his sister were standing. "You hear what he said," he shouted. "You hear the major!"

"We heard him, Chico," Annalisa told him, smiling at her brother's excitement. Then she looked over his head and her smile became shy and uncertain, for Sergeant Missouri was crossing the courtyard toward them.

Standing beside the group, he leaned lightly on the little donkey's back to ease the strain on his right leg. For a moment all were silent. . . . In the warm spring sunlight they stood quietly together, the thoughts in their hearts too subtle—or perhaps too simple—for easy speech.

Finally, Chico spoke, trying hard to find the right words. "Sergeant Missouri," he said, "now that Sergeant Donkey is out of the Army—will you come to see him often, at our house?"

The sergeant nodded, his eyes very blue and direct in his tanned young face. "Of course, Chico. A friend is a friend. I plan to visit Sergeant Donkey often. In fact, I'd like to come tonight." He was talking to the boy, but looking at Annalisa for an answer.

"I am at home tonight," she said softly.

Sergeant Missouri looked down at the little donkey, standing so patiently, his silver-sandy eyelashes making him look half-asleep in the sun. With a faint, musing expression on his face, the American removed the Purple Heart from his tunic and pinned it to the halter of the donkey's bridle.

"Congratulations, Sergeant," he said. "It belongs to both of us."

About the Author

Maureen Daly has been a well-known name to young readers ever since her first novel *Seventeenth Summer* was published in 1942. Her writing career got off to an auspicious start when at age 16 her short story *Sixteen* won first prize in Scholastic Magazine's short story contest and was selected for the O. Henry Best Short Stories Collection the same year. Her most recent novels include *Acts of Love* and *Promises to Keep* from Scholastic Books. Maureen Daly now lives in California.

LIVING HISTORY LIBRARY

The *Living History Library* is a collection of works for children published by Bethlehem Books, comprising quality reprints of historical fiction and non-fiction, including biography. These books are chosen for their craftsmanship and for the intelligent insight they provide into the present, in light of events and personalities of the past.

TITLES IN THIS SERIES

Archimedes and the Door of Science, by Jeanne Bendick

Augustine Came to Kent, by Barbara Willard

Beowulf the Warrior, by Ian Serraillier

The Hidden Treasure of Glaston, by Eleanore M. Jewett

Hittite Warrior, by Joanne Williamson

If All the Swords in England, by Barbara Willard

Madeleine Takes Command, by Ethel C. Brill

The Reb and the Redcoats, by Constance Savery

Red Hugh, Prince of Donegal, by Robert T. Reilly

The Small War of Sergeant Donkey, by Maureen Daly

Son of Charlemagne, by Barbara Willard

The Winged Watchman, by Hilda van Stockum